A Collection of Inspirational Short Stories from the Heart of the North Carolina Mountains

By Julianne Kuykendall Rhodes

Copyright June 2019

Book Dedication

This book is dedicated to my sweet husband, Wayne, who continually encourages my writing! Love you!

Author's Note

Dear Readers:

Thank you very much for taking the time to read this collection of short stories. These seven stories are very sentimental to me as they represent my first attempts at writing fiction. My prayer is that these stories inspire people. If any of these stories have inspired you in any way, could you drop me a line at julianne8235@yahoo.com? I would love to hear from you!

Enjoy!

Julianne Kuykendall Rhodes

"The Winning Season"

When Jessie Rogers was a junior at Pisgah High School in the small paper mill mountain town of Canton, North Carolina, he lived for baseball. Standing six foot, two inches, he had curly dark brown hair and deep green eyes and boasted a strong, taut build – and he was really good at baseball. However, he wasn't as good as he wanted to be – and he never felt he was good enough for his father, Bryce Rogers, who always wanted to have a superstar baseball player for a son. While his father cheered from the stands, Jessie could always see the disappointed look in his eyes when he struck out or when his team lost a game.

During one game when Jessie had tried

particularly hard to "knock one out of the park," he struck out and the only thing he knocked out of the park was his team's chance of a winning season that year during his junior year. His dad hung his head and drove him home in silence. That night, Jessie overheard his dad tell his mother, "I just wish my son could have one winning season. Is that too much to ask?"

After Jessie heard that comment, he became determined to give his dad a winning season that next year – his final chance as a senior in high school. He vigorously practiced batting and catching and kept himself in tip-top physical shape for a year. Then, around the middle of the season, he had almost worn himself out physically, and, as a result, busted his knee so severely that his coach had to take him out of the game for the rest of the season.

He was so depressed. Now his dad would never get his winning season.

After high school, Jessie missed baseball so much that he decided to coach a Little League baseball team. "Maybe I can get my winning season this way," he thought as he signed up to coach who he knew was a very talented team of 10-year-old boys.

He could quickly tell these boys were really, really fantastic.

Unfortunately, though, there was one little boy on the team, Blade, who always managed to throw the game off enough for the team to lose. Most of the boys had played baseball since their 3-year-old t-ball days, but this blond-headed kid had never played at all until that season.

The kid was terrible.

He couldn't bat. He couldn't catch. He was clumsy and nervous out on the field. His mistakes had cost the team several games but Jessie had to let him play equally according to the Little League rules, so Jessie just hung his head in silence when Blade cost the team another game and ran to meet his mother, Julia, who greeted her son with a warm hug no matter how badly he had played. Julia was always alone and showed up at the games a little late, wearing her medical scrubs from the local nursing home where she worked as a nurse's aide. She always smiled big at Jessie while her eyes – the bluest eyes he had ever seen – lit up like a Christmas tree in clear admiration for Blade, so Jessie mustered up a slight smile for the woman even though he felt like asking her to spare the team and take her son home.

Since he couldn't do that either, Jessie decided to practice with Blade one-on-one for an afternoon.

It was just the two of them.

They spent a warm spring afternoon together while Jessie gave him extra help in swinging to hit the ball, and threw the ball back and forth to Blade for a couple of hours to help with his catching. After all, the next game would determine if the season was a winning season or a losing season.

The next game, Blade was a much better player and wore a confident smile when he stepped up to bat. After missing the ball twice, he remembered what Jessie had told him the day before and focused as hard as he could on the ball and swung the bat with all his might. Jessie couldn't believe it when he saw the baseball clear the fence. Blade had scored a home run!

Jessie ran and found the ball and signed it with the words "Home Run Ball" and handed it to Blade right then and there.

Blade grinned from ear to ear. In his whole life, Jessie had never seen a boy so happy. In that moment, he saw the sheer love of the game born in Blade – something Jessie had lost along the way.

During the last inning, however, when the game was still so close it was anybody's game, Blade missed a crucial outfield catch and threw it so awkwardly that it blew by the first baseman, giving clearance for three runs for the other team which landed them victory in that game.

Jessie could still remember how defeated his own father looked in the stands when he realized that the winning season just slipped out of grasp.

"I can't even have a winning season in Little League – I'm officially a failure," Jessie thought as he cleaned up the field and watched his players trickle off to their cars with their families.

After that, he forgot all about baseball and focused his mind on opening up his own car dealership business and making as much money as possible which he did for the next 20 years of his life. When he was 39 years old, he stopped by his mailbox at the end of the cul-de-sac driveway leading to his very comfortable two-story home where he then lived in Charlotte, North Carolina. Kids and baseball was the farthest thing from his mind when he opened up a box that read "Blade Kendall" on the Canton, North Carolina return address.

Curiously, he opened the box and discovered a worn, tattered old baseball in it with faded magic marker writing that once clearly read, "Home Run Ball."

With the baseball came a note that simply read, "Mr. Jessie Rogers – my name is Blade Kendall. I don't know if you remember me or not but you were my baseball coach when I was 10 years old. That was the only year I played baseball. My mom was a single mom and couldn't afford for me to play anymore after that. I just wanted to let you know that the afternoon you spent with me was the best day of my life as a kid. I never knew my dad, but, that day, you were my dad. I know I wasn't very good at baseball, but the day you gave me this home run ball was the proudest moment of my childhood and I wanted you to have it back. I'm still not much good at baseball but I have a 5-year-old son, Keavon, now, and I'm coaching him and his first baseball team. We are all having a ball out there on the field. Here is a picture of the team – I thought you would like it. Thank you again, Blade."

As Jessie placed the threadbare, ragged baseball on his mantle along with the note and the team picture of about 15 dirty, smiling faces of 5-year-old baseball players just having fun with the game, he had big tears in his eyes when he realized one very important thing.

Twenty years ago – although the scoreboard didn't reflect it – he already truly had a "winning season."

\

"Two 'Angels' on a Bus"

Eighteen-year-old Mandolin Rhodes stood impatiently in line at the Greyhound bus station in Florence, South Carolina. At the end of the line of about 30 passengers with bus tickets in hand, she placed her two overnight bags on the hot pavement and pulled her blond hair up in a ponytail in a futile attempt to withstand the sweltering late August heat.

What was the hold up?

She was anxious to board the air-conditioned bus and get on her way to visit her aunt and uncle in the cool North Carolina mountains for Labor Day weekend, her first long overdue mini-vacation in two years.

Then she saw him.

In about the middle of the line, a straggly man who looked to be in his 50s and who clearly looked homeless was attempting to board the Greyhound bus alongside his equally straggly-looking mutt of a dog with a rope around its neck as a makeshift leash. Beside the pair was a large cardboard box that held his belongings.

"There's no way in the world they are gonna let that man and his dog on that bus," Mandolin muttered to herself, her patience growing more and more thin with every minute the homely-looking man attempted to negotiate with the bus driver.

Suddenly, the bus driver shouted to the crowd, "Everybody stand back – I'm going to let this gentleman and his service dog on first!"

"Seriously? A service dog?"

Mandolin didn't even try to keep her words quiet as other bus passengers chimed in on their frustration.

"A service dog has identification on them dude – not a freaking rope!" one guy with a thick Yankee accent shouted in front of Mandolin while others sighed in clear exasperation.

Yet, nothing altered the bus driver's firm decision.

After the man and his "service dog" boarded the very back of the bus, the other passengers trickled on slowly, showing the bus driver their tickets before boarding.

As Mandolin handed her ticket to the bus driver, she saw an unmistakable kindness in his blue eyes, and figured the kind bus driver had mercy on the man, letting his dog ride along with the knowingly false rationalization that the dog was a service dog, the only type of dogs permitted on the bus.

Something about the bus driver's kind blue eyes reminded Mandolin of the blue eyes and the kindness and faith of her father and mother, who had died together two years earlier.

As she stepped on the bus, a Bible verse that her parents asked her to repeat every day of her life popped into her mind: "Seek ye first the kingdom of God and His righteousness and all these things shall be added unto you."

Immediately, she dismissed the thought.

"I don't want to think about that verse," thought Mandolin, huffing. "What good did it do my parents?"

The Bible verse continually echoed through her heart and she shrugged it off every time as she made her way down the bus aisles, looking for an empty seat. The other passengers had clearly tried to avoid the homeless man and his dog at the back of the bus and had taken up every seat away from them.

"Are you kidding me?" thought Mandolin when she discovered that the only seat available on the whole bus was the second to the last seat, right in front of the homeless man and his dog.

The horrible stench of body odor and wet dog coming from the back of the bus almost made Mandolin throw up. The thick cough the man had didn't help matters at all.

With no other choice, she plopped down in the only empty seat and covered her nose with her t-shirt.

"This is gonna be a long ride to Asheville," she said, plugging her cell phone charger into the electrical outlet in front of her seat, putting in her ear buds and staring out the bus window, wishing the bus to get going.

As the bus pulled out of the Florence bus station, the driver's voice was heard over the speaker. "Welcome aboard Greyhound, next stop is Sumter," he said loud and clear.

Mandolin tried to listen to YouTube music, and then she tried to take a nap, but she grew more and more restless. That Bible verse kept rattling through her mind and heart: "Seek ye first the kingdom of God and His righteousness and all these things shall be added unto you."

Mandolin hadn't talked to God in two years but she did then. "God, could you please get that verse out of my mind? I really don't want to hear it."

She still believed in God, she guessed, but she was taking a break right now, still too mad at God for taking two of the nicest people on this earth – her parents Jessie and Kathryn Rhodes.

She was bitter, angry and resentful.

She was a 16-year-old only child two years ago on that fateful Friday, riding in the back cab of her father's Ford pickup and her parents were in the front. It was the NASCAR Southern 500 race in Darlington that Labor Day weekend and she had rode with her father to pick up her mother where she worked in the racetrack museum and gift shop. They had just pulled out of the museum parking lot when her father saw a drunk guy beating up his girlfriend on the side of the road where they were camping before the big race.

As he watched the guy shove his girlfriend up again his white Dodge Ram pickup and smack her repeatedly across the face, he impulsively pulled his truck over in an attempt to rescue the girl.

"Don't you touch her again!" Jessie shouted to the guy, putting a finger up in his face, while his wife tried to pull Jessie away from the domestic violence scene.

Her father was a good and peaceful man and would never start a fight with anyone, but he would stand up for anyone in distress in a heartbeat.

"You and your woman get out of here and go on down the road – this is none of your business," the drunk guy with a beer in his hand exclaimed, kicking dirt on Jessie.

"It IS my business and I'm calling for help," Jessie retorted back as he and Kathryn quickly made their way back to their truck.

That would be the final words Jessie would ever say.

They didn't know what had hit them when the drunk guy angrily pulled out a pistol and began firing random shots which killed them both.

While the guy and his girlfriend pulled off in a fury, leaving behind a trail of smoke, Mandolin desperately called "911" and cradled her parents in her arms, watching them take their last breaths.

The guy was eventually caught somewhere in Myrtle Beach and she had to be a witness in court against him to receive a life sentence for the double murder.

That's why Mandolin was so mad at God right now – for taking her parents for just trying to be Good Samaritans to a girl on the side of the road. Even though she knew somehow that her parent's strong faith and her faith would bring her back to God someday, she didn't want it to be today.

Someday...but not today.

Without any life insurance and no significant savings passed down to her, Mandolin had to grow up real fast as a 16-year-old only child. After her parent's meager savings paid for their double funeral and got her by for a couple months, she was forced to quit school and landed a waitress job at Cain's BBQ.

She had done the math.

She needed to make $80 in tips at least five days a week to get by on just the basics she needed without going into foster care. It wasn't much, but she got by.

The only reason she had enough money for the bus ticket was because she had worked an extra shift at the restaurant.

She just had to get out of town this Labor Day weekend – she couldn't handle being anywhere near Darlington during race time when she was continually reminded of her parent's untimely death.

So, no, she wasn't in the best of moods. And she might turn back to God someday, but it couldn't be today. Not this Labor Day weekend filled with tragic memories.

Slumping in her seat further, she had settled on that decision and blocked the Bible verse out of her mind, at least temporarily.

Still, the verse re-played in her mind until she gave in.

"Ok, God...what do you want me to do? Why did you take my parents? Can't you see I'm hurting here?" Mandolin asked.

Just then, she felt a strong urging in her heart from God just to turn around and talk to the homeless man. The words "Just ask him his name" kept coming to her mind.

Finally, because she was pretty much stuck and really had nothing else better to do on the bus ride, she turned around and saw a skinny man with shaggy brown hair and green eyes who looked and smelled like he hadn't bathed in at least a solid month. It was then, though, that she noticed what he was doing. He was reading a small green New Testament Bible.

"So what's your name?" Mandolin asked the man.

Clearly in shock, the man looked up from his Bible and stumbled over his words, shuffling around in his seat.

"Uh, ummm...Brad. My name is Brad," he answered.

"So where are you going?"

"I'm on my way to Columbia," he answered again.

"So what are you doing in Columbia for Labor Day?" Mandolin asked.

"Well, it's kind of a long story – you probably don't really want to know," Brad said, his head down a bit.

Mostly out of boredom, Mandolin was curious now, especially since he was reading the Bible – the Bible her parents taught her and lived by.

"I've got time," she said.

"Well, if you really want to know....um, I'm sick," Brad started.

He paused a long time, as if trying to form the words – the words that, once spoken, would make his situation more real.

Finally, he just blurted it out.

"I've got lung cancer and I don't have long – I haven't seen my mother in 30 years but she told me I could come to her house in Columbia so that's why I'm going there."

Wow.

For once in her life, Mandolin was completely speechless.

That's why the man was so skinny. That's why the man was coughing. That's apparently why the bus driver had let him and his "service dog" on the bus in the first place.

"So you're going to Columbia to die?" she asked after a long pause.

"Yeah, pretty much I guess...doctor says I've got a week or two."

"Oh my goodness, I'm so very sorry," Mandolin sincerely expressed to the stranger behind her who had suddenly become her friend in the span of five minutes.

"Thank you."

"So is that why you're reading the Bible?" she questioned.

"Yeah...when I was real little, my mother took me to church every once in a while, pretty much for a babysitter for a couple hours, but I remember my Sunday School teacher gave me this Bible and told me that if I ever wanted to be saved to talk to her," he told. "I never went back to that church much after that because we moved around a lot so I really don't know how to be saved but I know I need to before I die."

So it was all out there.

Mandolin knew instinctively what she needed to do – what she had to do.

She had to turn back to God herself so she could help this man.

She had not planned on turning back to God today, but apparently it was God's plan.

"God, please forgive me for turning away from you and please give me the words to help this poor man," Mandolin prayed.

"I can help you," she then simply stated to Brad.

Then, she took the man's Bible and showed him the Bible verses called the

"Roman's Road" like her parents had taught her to do and led him in his salvation prayer. She prayed the words and he repeated after her, right there at the back of the bus: "Dear God, I know I'm a sinner, and I ask for your forgiveness. I believe Jesus Christ is Your Son. I believe that He died for my sin and that you raised Him to life. I want to trust Him as my Savior and follow him as Lord, from this day forward. Guide my life and help me to do your will. I pray this in the name of Jesus. Amen."

Mandolin didn't think she had ever seen so much happiness in a person's face as she did when Brad lifted his face after that prayer.

His tired green eyes showed an unmistakable joy that had been missing before – an eternal joy that said this world was not his home but that he was ready for his heavenly home.

For the rest of the ride to Columbia, she told him about her parent's tragic death and he told her about his chemotherapy treatments that he had recently refused to take anymore and how nervous he was so see his mother again after all this time and she gave him advice.

"Just talk and talk and talk to her – tell her all about your life and the Bible that your teacher gave you and how it eventually led you to God," Mandolin advised. "Don't waste a minute, but just talk to her."

Brad assured her he would.

"Ok, this stop is Columbia," the bus driver spoke loudly over the intercom, as Brad stood up to leave.

As he prepared to depart the bus, she gave him a side hug and said simply, "When you get to heaven, tell my parents I said hello and that I'm ok now."

Brad's smile held an otherworldly peace about it at the thought.

"I sure will," he declared before he walked off the bus, pausing to wave goodbye before heading into the bus stop.

Mandolin cried much of the way from Columbia to Asheville that day, but it wasn't tears of sadness – it was tears of joy.

She felt more joy than she had in two years.

God had brought together two unlikely strangers on a bus to be each other's "angels" that day on the bus and, while she might have had a hand in saving Brad's life that day, he had also saved hers.

Brad came to God that day, but Mandolin came back.

Mandolin ended up staying in Asheville with her aunt and uncle, going back to school and eventually working in guest relations at the Billy Graham Training Center at The Cove in Asheville where she was able to share with many people about God and how to be saved and have peace with God. She also set up a domestic violence shelter called "Mandolin's House" in memory of her parents to help those in abusive domestic situations just like the girl her parents died for trying to help.

Five years later when she met and married a man she met at The Cove in a beautiful mountain summer wedding, she missed her parents immensely but she could almost hear them whisper down to her from heaven: "Seek ye first the kingdom of God and His righteousness and all these things shall be added unto you."

"The Biggest Tip at the Jukebox Junction"

Callie Anderson rushed into the Jukebox Junction on Friday after school, pulling on her serving apron as she went.

She was supposed to be there at 3:15 p.m. It was 3:38.

"You're late again, Callie – that makes the second time this week," her manager, Steve, called out to her in his half-joking friend way, half-serious manager way as he rang up a customer at the cash register.

"I'm sorry, it's crazy trying to get out of the parking lot after school," Callie responded, clocking in.

She wore blue jeans, tennis shoes and a Jukebox Junction white t-shirt and pulled her long, pretty brown hair into a Pisgah Bears ball cap and threw on some silver hoop earrings and pink lip gloss to start her shift.

"Well don't you look cute," her co-worker Slade commented, cooking up curly fries the restaurant was locally known for.

A rush of heat hit Callie's cheeks, but she hid it well. At 16, it was exciting to be complimented by a hot 25-year-old.

"Cute and late," Callie quipped back while Slade laughed. "Not a good combination if I want to keep this job."

Her first table was two local police officers. One ordered a stir-fry and the other a Chuck wagon sandwich and curly fries. Both ordered Java chocolate milkshakes.

"Great, at least they'll give me a good tip," Callie muttered under her breath while she put their order in via touch screen on the computer.

Police officers always tipped well and she relied on her tips since she turned 16.

At home, it was just Callie and her mother, Clarissa, who many people mistook for her sister rather than her mother. At just 31 years old, Clarissa took great care of herself and didn't look much older than her spunky daughter.

The short story Callie had always heard was that her mother was 15 and her father was 17 when she was born and her grandfather had thrown her father out of the hospital when he came to see her when she was a newborn.

"He works at Hardee's for goodness sake!" her grandfather had shouted at her mother. "His family is trash and he will never have anything...I will make sure he's never around you again!"

The only thing Callie knew about him was that he had a tattoo of angel wings on his right arm. "His mother had died in a car accident when he was little and he always said she was his guardian angel," her mother had told her one day on a summer walk along the Pigeon River.

The wistful way she said it, Callie guessed her mother still loved him deep down because she never seemed to give her heart to anyone else.

So, anyways, it was just Callie and her mother and they did okay.

Her mother worked as a C.N.A. at the local nursing home and kept the mortgage paid and food on the table. However, when Callie turned 16, she let her know if she wanted her own phone and car and clothes, she would have to be responsible for them.

That's why the tips were so important to Callie. Her car payment for her Honda Accord was due this week and she needed another $75 to pay it.

The policemen were just leaving and left $8 each on the table for Callie.

"See you for breakfast in the morning Callie," one of the policemen yelled, with a quick wave as he walked out the door, holding it open for a second for another customer walking in.

"Sure thing...I'll have your biscuits and gravy ready for you," Callie called back.

Just as she was wiping down the policemen's table, another two men started to sit down at the same table.

"Let me just wipe this table off for you and I'll be right back for your drink order," Callie politely greeted the two men.

"Okay little gal, we're really hungry so we might just go ahead and order if you don't mind," said the taller of the two men, as they sat down.

"Sure...I'd be happy to take your order now."

"What's your special?"

"Our special is mountain trout...we have that on the weekends with all the fixin's," Callie answered.

"Now that sounds good for two hungry men – we'll take you up on that."

So it was settled. The two men both ordered a large mountain trout meal, ice water and large chocolate milkshakes.

While the men ate their trout, hushpuppies, slaw and salad, Callie casually asked where they were from.

The tall man answered. "Well, this is my buddy from over the hill in Andrews. I haven't seen him in a long time and we're catching up."

"So, what about you? Where are you from?"

"I live in Wyoming – got a few cattle out there. Visiting an old buddy and seeing the countryside here."

"Well, I hope you enjoy your visit," she responded courteously with a smile.

When the pair were almost finished inhaling the chocolate milkshakes, the tall man motioned Callie over to the table.

"Little girl, what's the biggest tip you've ever got here?"

"Well, ummm...I guess it was $50," Callie thought back. "Yes it was a $50 bill a couple gave me at Christmas."

"$50 huh?"

"Yeah, why do you ask?"

"Well, I thought I would leave you a million dollars...how would you like that tip?"

Callie laughed at the joke.

"Yeah, a million dollar tip would be nice, but I don't think that'll ever happen," she quickly retorted, wiping off a nearby table with a white cloth and sliding three $1 bills into her serving apron.

The two men thanked her profusely for the delicious trout she recommended and trickled off to the restroom before she saw them leaving in a beat up Ford pickup truck with a Wyoming license plate.

When she went back to the table to gather up their dishes and wipe off their table, she looked for a few dollars in cash but there was nothing.

"That's really odd," thought Callie.

Then, she saw the check. Instead of cash, the tall man had left a check.

Called laughed again when she saw the check was made out for a million dollars. "Oh my goodness...he wrote me a fake check and then stiffed me," thought Callie.

Aggravated, she almost ripped up the check but decided to show it to Slade instead. Slade would get a good laugh out of it, she thought.

"What in the world Callie? I know you're cute and all, but seriously? A million dollars?" Slade teased Callie as she threw away the paper plates and cups in the kitchen.

Then, Slade took a second look at the check. "Callie, this has your last name on here. How did he know your last name?"

"What?" Callie asked as she looked the check over again.

"I didn't tell him my last name, no. My nametag just says 'Callie.'"

"Well, maybe you should call and see if it's real, just for the fun of it," Slade suggested.

"They would totally laugh at me over the phone."

Then, Callie thought again about that last name. How did he know her last name?

"That's so weird," Callie thought as she pulled her cell phone out of her apron and called Wells Fargo that the check was written on.

"You better hurry. It's 4:47 and the bank closes at 5," Slade reminded her, looking over her shoulder at the check.

A kind bank teller answered the phone as Callie and Slade listened on speaker phone. "Wells Fargo...this is Grace how may I help you?"

Callie didn't exactly know how to ask this. "Hi this is Callie Anderson. I know you can't tell me any details but can you tell me if you can cash a check from a certain account?"

"Sure, darling. What's the account number and the amount?"

Callie called off the account number and then hesitated. "It's written for a million dollars," Callie said with a laugh. "I'm pretty sure it's a joke I'm just checking."

"Can I put you a brief hold while I check that account?" Grace asked.

"Sure."

When Grace clicked back on the phone, Callie could almost see her smiling through the phone.

"Miss Anderson are you still there?"

"Yes mam."

"Sweetie, you'll have no problem cashing that check."

Callie and Slade's jaws both dropped open. It was only then that Callie saw a certain symbol in the left hand corner of that check and her hand flew up to her mouth.

The symbol was angel's wings.

"Jordan's Dance"

Jordan Ray woke up to Taylor Swift's "Shake it Off" song at 6 a.m. that bitter cold Thursday morning in January when the alarm on her iPhone went off. Immediately, she clicked on the weather app on her phone and checked the weather.

A single white snowflake still appeared beside the word Friday, just like it had all day the day before. "Seriously? It can't snow tomorrow!" Jordan shrieked to her father, who was calmly reading the newspaper at the kitchen table as she marched by on her way to the bathroom for her morning shower.

"Why did you have to move me up to this Hickville place?" Jordan screamed before she slammed the bathroom door.

"Oh, so now the snow is my fault too?" her father retorted back to her. "Yeah, that seems logical."

The back and forth snippy banter between progressive financial planner William Ray and his 16-year-old daughter Jordan had become their new normal since the summer before when he was transferred within his company from their Charlotte, North Carolina headquarters to the Asheville, North Carolina office.

William and his wife, Lora, had dreamed about moving to the North Carolina mountains one day, so they looked at this transfer opportunity as a blessing from God to make their move a little sooner in life.

Unfortunately, their 16-year-old daughter Jordan who entered her junior year at a new mountain high school didn't quite see the mountains as a blessing from God. To her, the mountains smothered her more like a jail cell, keeping her away from the city life in Charlotte and the friends she had known all of her life.

"Just give her a little time, she'll be ok," Lora commented, trying her best to comfort her husband as she gave him a kiss on the cheek.

Neither parent was convinced of that, however, as they listened to their only daughter cry her eyes out in the shower. The only thing that her brightened Jordan's spirits at all since last summer was being invited to the high school's Winter Formal which was supposed to happen that Friday night in the school's gym.

Snow in the weather forecast threatened to overshadow even her sliver of happiness.

Jordan stood in front of the bathroom mirror in a white towel, blankly staring in the mirror as she brushed her long, brown hair.

"Why in the world does it have to snow on the day of the dance?" thought Jordan, who loved music and loved to dance on the weekends back with her friends in Charlotte. "There was finally something halfway cool going on up here and now it has to snow."

Walking into the high school dressed like an Old Navy model with her chunky winter sweater, leggings and dress boots and her hair and makeup on perfect point, Jordan spotted her Winter Formal date, Nate.

"Hey pretty girl," Nate greeted her with a smile. "Good morning."

"Good morning Nate."

Jordan had to admit he was a good looking guy, even though she labeled him as a redneck when she took a quick picture of him and Snapchatted it to her friends back home.

The Snapchat picture was of him at a church Christmas party, dressed in a plaid flannel shirt, jeans, hiking boots and a camouflaged ball cap. One of the girls in the church's youth group had thrown on a red and white Santa hat on top of the camouflaged cap so she labeled the picture "Redneck Santa."

Her best friend Kristen snapped, "He's hot."

Jordan had to agree her friend was right, but she couldn't admit it – couldn't let herself get too attached.

"Whatever lol...get me out of here!" Jordan lightheartedly commented back to her best friend.

Nate looked out the school window towards the looming snow clouds. "The weatherman says five inches of snow after midnight tonight but it sure looks like it's coming sooner than tonight and a lot more. I think they pegged that wrong," Nate commented.

"Better get your snow boots out city girl," he teased Jordan.

Annoyed, Jordan rolled her eyes. "Can you just drive me back to Charlotte, like now?"

"Come on, we hicks up here aren't so bad are we?" Nate said playfully, trying to keep the conversation cheerful. He had fallen head over heels for Jordan the minute he met her at their church's youth Sunday School class yet Jordan hadn't really fallen for him, though.

In fact, the only reason she had agreed to go to the dance with him was to escape boredom and because he had asked her to go to the dance when he spelled out "Winter Dance?" in whipped cream on an oversized red plastic plate at their youth group Christmas party.

How could she really have said "No" to that?

"Whatever...I just don't belong here," she quipped back to Nate before they began trickling off to their separate first period classes.

"I'll pick you up at 6 p.m. sharp tomorrow night for the dance, ok?" Nate asked quickly before she was out of sight.

"Ok I guess if we still have it," Jordan flatly responded.

However, before her first period class was even over, Principal Henson's voice came over loud and clear on the intercom. "Good morning Pisgah High School. Sorry for this interruption but we wanted to go ahead and inform all students and teachers that we will begin dismissing school at 10 this morning due to the incoming inclement weather. Also, the Winter Formal committee has made the decision to cancel tomorrow night's dance for now and they will reschedule at a later date to be determined. Everyone stay safe out there and have a great weekend."

And, just like that, Jordan's somewhat high spirit from a couple days before was totally deflated.

"I'm really sorry about the dance," Nate immediately texted, then followed with a second text: "You still wanna go when they have it?"

"I doubt I'll still be living here then," Jordan texted back.

"Don't let a little snow scare you away," Nate teased in his next text.

Jordan didn't feel like texting anymore so she just responded with a short "lol" and the texting conversation was over.

When she pulled her Ford Fusion up to her parent's log home on Dix Creek Road in the Bethel community of Haywood County just west of Asheville, she could already see snow flurries.

She crashed on their sectional sofa in the living room and mindlessly watched television for a couple of hours until her parents came home from work, carrying groceries and flashlights and candles with them in preparation for being snowed in.

"Look here, we are going to get to experience our first real mountain snow as a family Jordan, isn't this great?" her father optimistically asked, kicking a little snow off of his black dress shoes at the front door while her mother put away groceries.

"No this isn't great, my life is one big disaster," Jordan snipped dramatically from the sofa.

Heavy snow began falling that Thursday evening as the temperatures dropped and snow fell throughout the night. Jordan woke up the next morning to a foot of snow and, by noon that Friday, two feet of snow blanketed their mountain property.

Her mother Lora just sat in her rocking chair and stared at the winter wonderland before her. It was Lora who had fallen in love with the particular place they had purchased last summer complete with a gorgeous view of the mountains and a creek providing natural mountain background music.

It was about 25 minutes from her husband's office in Asheville but she loved it and loved the church at the bottom of the hill – a pristine place to finish raising her daughter, she had decided. Plus, her daughter would have memories of church youth group summer camps instead of witnessing all the rising Charlotte crime.

"Look at this Jordan...isn't this the prettiest thing you've ever seen?" her mother honestly asked.

"No it's not pretty at all, it's trapping me here," Jordan said, even though she couldn't help but take a picture of the snow and post it on her Facebook page for her friends to see.

"I'm jealous," her friend Christy had commented and Jordan had replied "Don't be...I just want out of here." Her friend had responded with a "Ha Ha" reaction to her

Facebook comment, but it was joke to Jordan when, about that time, all the power in the house suddenly went off due to the heavy snow and Jordan realized she just had two percent of power on her phone.

"What in the world?" Jordan shouted to her phone, while she barely heard her father saying something about getting a generator out of the basement, giving her hope that she could plug up her dying phone with the help of a generator.

After her father got their generator going, he explained that the generator could only power two things and they needed it for the refrigerator and a light so she would have to wait to plug up her phone.

He proudly heated the house with a small kerosene heater he sat in the kitchen.

"Okay, my life is officially over now," Jordan informed her parents, then shot off a quick text to Nate, who lived about three miles down the road.

"Soooo our power is out and my phone is about dead so just letting you know in case you try to text."

"Yeah our power is out too...too many trees on the lines I guess...try to enjoy it," Nate texted back before Jordan's phone went completely black.

Her father, in his usual upbeat, optimistic spirit, suggested, "This would be a superb time for board games, how about it Jordan? Want to try to beat your father in Monopoly? I bet you can't!"

"No I don't...I'm not a child anymore, Dad."

"Well, you don't have to be a child to play Monopoly, do you? Come on, we can all play."

"That's ok...I'm just gonna sit here and close my eyes and try to transport myself back home," Jordan replied, slumping on the sofa and burying her head in her hands and began to openly sob.

However, this time the teenage snarkiness was gone. Instead, Jordan wept like a small child just homesick for something familiar, while her mother and father sat down on either side of her on the sofa with their arms around her.

"I've tried to like it here, I really have but this is just not me up here...I just don't belong here," Jordan expressed to her parents through sobs. "Can we please just go back home, please?"

William and Lora just looked at each other not knowing what to say to comfort their daughter.

Her mother was the first to speak.

"Sweetie, maybe...maybe this was our dream and it wasn't your dream. Maybe we should have waited at least until you were out of high school to make the move," Lora began, rubbing her daughter's back.

Her father chimed in. "We had the best of intentions, really we did, Jordan. We love you, do you know that?"

"Yes I know, but I just can't do this up here and with this snow...I'm just at the end of my rope."

William thought long and hard and looked at his daughter. As much of a professional as he was, he realized that his higher calling was that of a father.

"I'll tell you what Jordan. I'll pray about it and I'll talk with my boss when the snow clears and see if I can work out of Charlotte for a couple more years. I will at least make the phone call and see what can be worked out...does that make you feel any better?"

"Yeah, some." Jordan was still crying when she said it but her father could tell he was getting through to her – that she knew he cared about her.

For the rest of the afternoon, the family just hung out in the living room together in comfy pajamas and kept warm due to the kerosene heater in the adjoining kitchen and watched the last of the snow fall before darkness closed in around 5:30 that Friday evening.

Then, as a family, they huddled around the kerosene heater as they ate a supper of a pre-cooked ham from the refrigerator and cold green beans and corn from the cabinet.

Jordan was about finished with her supper when she heard movement outside in their yard. It was a little eerily still and quiet with the power out on the mountain so Jordan had no idea what the noise could be.

Suddenly, there was a loud knock on their front door.

Her father opened the door to see an absolutely frozen Nate Richards standing on their front porch, looking like an Eskimo dressed from head to toe in Carhartt overalls, thick gloves, hiking boots and a wool winter hat with flaps over his ears.

As frozen as he was, though, the boy still had an awkward smile and surprisingly, one plastic red rose in his hand.

"Well hello young man – good to see you," her father greeted Nate as the two shook hands.

Jordan was still in her comfy pajamas she had received as a Christmas gift when she made it to the door.

"I believe we have a dance to go to, Miss Jordan," Nate spoke loud and clear yet clearly still shivering from the cold.

"May I have this dance?" he politely asked Jordan as he handed her the red rose.

Then, she looked at the clock. It was 6 o'clock on the dot. That boy had trudged three miles in two feet of snow just to pick her up and dance with her like he had promised.

As cold as the mountain air was, her heart had never felt so warm.

"You walked all the way up here in the snow to dance with me?" she asked, her mouth open.

"Yes, I sure did...so are you gonna take a freezing boy in and dance with him or not?"

"Come on in," Jordan replied, laughing.

Then, with no music at all and just the rhythm of their skipping heartbeats to guide their dance, typically high maintenance Jordan still in her pajama pants danced with a frigid Nate still sporting his Carhartts while her parents watched from the living room.

"No one has ever done anything this nice for me in my whole life," Jordan told Nate.

"Well, we mountain boys might not be so bad after all," Nate shot back, twirling her around in the kitchen.

Her parents couldn't hide their smiles and her father asked, with his teasing eyes twinkling, "Jordan, do you still want me to make that phone call?"

"I think we can wait on that phone call a little while," responded Jordan, with her head on Nate's shoulder and enjoying the few minutes of the dance, certain she would never quite feel this special again in her whole life.

"Rose's Cold Walk on Interstate 40"

It was my idea to go out to eat in Asheville that brutal cold night in January. It was supposed to be the coldest air of the winter – just a measly 5 degrees with a wind chill factor of -10 degrees in the mountains of North Carolina.

The frigid cold reflected my five-year marriage – cold, barren, loveless – but, for some reason that night, I thought maybe I could save my marriage to Jackson.

Like a miracle was awaiting.

I thought maybe the problems in our marriage were all my fault like he always twisted them around to be – maybe if I had a better attitude or was a little sexier or if our 3-

year-old daughter Samantha didn't pester him so much or...

My thoughts came to a screeching halt when I saw it in the mirror.

There it was – it was too visible to ignore. A giant bruise on my right thigh.

"My word...I had no idea that was there."

The night before, Jackson had been hammering bookcases together – bookcases that, ironically, he had pushed over the week before that in a violent rage, spilling books and photo albums across the living room floor.

While he was nailing the bookcases back together, I had told him that supper was hot and ready to eat.

"Why in the world do you push me so much? Can't you let me do one thing without nagging me to no end?" he had screamed. "Can I not get any peace around this house?"

Like always – nothing I did was right and everything was always my fault in his eyes.

Then came the rage – and the flying hammer thrown randomly at my right thigh as he stormed out the front door.

I had rushed to console little Samantha who was crying in fear and I had almost forgotten about the pain from the hammer.

But the black and blue evidence was too much to ignore. I felt sick when I thought that, after his violent episode the night before when he came back home and profusely apologized, I had been intimate with him with that horrific, ugly bruise on my thigh.

I didn't want to, but I felt like I had to keep the peace and so he wouldn't think that I wanted to leave him.

One time when I had threatened to leave with Samantha, he pulled out a gas lighter and started burning a cardboard box, threatening to burn our house down if I left.

So, I pacified him and stayed for that night, trying to make a plan to leave safely. Then that night had bled into another week which had bled into another month which had bled into five years with this man who I feared leaving.

"What are you going to do Rose?" I asked myself as I stood in front of the full-length mirror, staring that the bruise that, unfortunately told the story of not only me, but the future of my daughter.

I was 28 years old. As I stood there looking at the mirror, I took a minute to remember ten years ago when I was like a blossoming 18-year-old red rose. That year, I was a gorgeous homecoming queen for goodness sake, not the withering red rose crushed on the ground who I barely recognized anymore.

I needed a miracle.

I wanted to leave, but what was I going to do? He controlled every penny of money. Once I had tried to wrap up the change he had thrown in a bucket every day by the front door. It was my plan to slowly gather up enough money to leave, money he wouldn't realize was gone. I had saved just $48 before he found the rolled coins in a Rubbermaid container in the back corner of our closet.

I had two black eyes after Jackson got through with me that night, and he threatened to kill me and my mother who lived alone if I ever tried to leave again. He even promised he would hunt me and Samantha down and anyone trying to protect us in any domestic violence shelter if we tried to go there.

After that night, I totally believed him.

He was evil enough to kill and I knew it.

So, what was I going to do as I looked at the young woman in the mirror? I didn't know what else to do except cover up the bruise and keep going. So I did just that. I dressed in a navy oversized sweater and brown leggings and boots for the cold weather and put on a fake smile.

I could do it for one more night while I decided what I would do.

Maybe Jackson would be in a good mood and we would actually have fun tonight for a change.

I was right.

When he walked in the front door, he was cheerful.

"Whewww, thank goodness," I muttered.

"We better bundle up real good tonight, it's gonna be freezing cold," I said in a sing-song way, trying to keep the mood positive as I zipped up my daughter's hot pink jacket, put her hood on and fitted her hands and fingers with pink and blue gloves.

Jackson scooped Samantha up walking out the door. "Come on my little snow angel," he had teased Samantha, but she cringed underneath his touch and desperately looked to me as we walked towards Jackson's old Chevy pickup.

I took Samantha's coat off and buckled her in her car seat in the center of the cab of the truck and we were soon on our way to Asheville. Jackson just stopped at the local gas station in Bethel for gas for his truck, talking to five people while he pumped gas.

"Hey buddy how you been?" some guy came up to him, shaking his hand as he pumped gas.

I waved politely at the man, all the while thinking how Jackson was a charmer and put up a good face in front of everyone else. No one would ever suspect what went on behind closed doors with us.

He was good at that, and reminded me often how no one would ever believe me if I told someone and asked for help.

Back in the truck as soon as he left the gas station parking lot, Jackson glared at me and demanded to know why I was flirting with his friend.

"I wasn't flirting, Jackson. The man waved at me and I waved back, that was all. What was I supposed to do, cross my arms and be rude to the man?"

"I'm married to a slut is all I know – you even dressed slutty for him. Why did you wear that? Jackson shot back at me.

I tried desperately to diffuse the situation.

"Jackson, I have on a nun looking oversized sweater that covers everything...how in the world is this slutty?"

I laughed and tried to brush the episode off.

"Don't you dare laugh at me. I know a slut when I see one and I'm married to one."

"Whatever, Jackson, you win. I'm tired of arguing with you."

The tension in the truck could be cut with a knife.

Samantha looked fearful and clung onto her orange stuffed basketball that she had made a pillow and come accustomed to sleeping with. She couldn't sleep without it now and named the basketball "Orangie."

Orangie somehow relaxed her when her father started raging.

Samantha had fallen asleep peacefully beside Orangie when they got on Interstate 40 in Candler headed towards Asheville.

"Where are we gonna eat?" I finally asked Jackson to hopefully break the icy tension.

"Well I was going to take you somewhere nice like the Olive Garden, but I think I'll just take a slut through the McDonald's drive thru."

When I started to cry, the insults just came sharper.

"Go ahead and cry like a wounded dog...my goodness, woman, can't you take a joke? Why do you have to be so weak?"

Jackson was impossible.

I had been sucked into the spiral of manipulation and I desperately wanted to get out.

About that time, I heard the unmistakable, sickening thud of a flat truck tire.

Jackson heard it too and pulled the truck sharply off the Interstate, cursing every breath and screaming at the flat tire.

"Did you do this to me? These are brand new tires! Did you purposely sabotage my tire so you could get away?" Jackson seethed.

"Seriously, Jackson? I'm continually amazed at how you can literally blame everything on me!"

I simply asked him if he could just change the tire so we could get on our way.

"Well, I would but you have the jack in your car, remember, from when I changed your tire last?"

His anger was flaring more and more, waking Samantha up from her deep sleep.

"You can't even be grateful for me changing a tire or be responsible enough to put the jack where it belongs!"

Jackson had a cell phone, although he wouldn't allow me to have one.

"Why don't you call the Highway Patrol? They can come out and help us quickly since it's so cold I hate to bother anyone else to come out tonight," I suggested.

"I'm not being a pansy and waiting on the Highway Patrol!" he hissed. "There's a weigh station about a mile up the road and there's always cops there and they can help me change the tire."

At that point, I got out of the truck and started getting Samantha out of her car seat. "Jackson, you're acting crazy! You can't possibly drive on this pavement with that tire – it's totally flat! The tire rim could catch fire on that pavement!"

"You don't even trust me to change a tire – you're the one who's crazy – just get your crap and get out of here then!"

I had never seen Jackson act so ridiculous in all the time we were married. The violence had gotten worse but this was on a whole new level.

I grabbed Samantha and my purse and tried to get our coats but there was no time. Jackson got his pocket knife and cut Orangie down the middle and threw the stuffed basketball out of the truck with its white stuffing blowing in the cold wind.

He would stop at nothing to be as cruel as he could be and get under my skin, I decided when I watched my daughter scream after Orangie and Jackson sped off on the side of the interstate with sparks flying underneath the bare tire rim on the pavement.

"He'll come back for us," I told Samantha, holding her tight and trying my best to comfort her while we both shivered to the bone in the cold, but deep inside I didn't want him to come back.

I wanted desperately to have my miracle.

With no cell phone and with cars and pickups and transfer trucks whizzing by on the busy interstate, I debated what in the world I would do. Samantha was inconsolable and I knew my first priority was to get her to safety, but I didn't even know exactly where I was and it was pitch dark.

I just had my sweater on because my coat and gloves were in the truck and Samantha was in the same predicament. I knew we had to get out of the cold quick.

Without knowing what else to do, I began walking furiously carrying my crying child and half of her stuffed basketball that was left, my anger somewhat warming my incredibly cold body and even colder heart.

I wanted to leave but, if I did, I knew he would find me. And what about my mother? I knew he would go after her.

Still I just kept walking. And then I started praying.

I hadn't prayed in years, but, suddenly, a Bible verse that I had learned when I was in Sunday School as a teenager flashed through my mind on that cold, lonely walk. It was from Jeremiah 29:11: "For I know the plans I have for you," declares the Lord, "plans to prosper you and not to harm you, plans to give you hope and a future."

I had been so hopeful when I recited that verse at church as a teenager, but somewhere, along the way, I had lost hope – like that verse didn't apply to me anymore.

I had let Jackson's negative words replace God's word and I had started to believe Jackson's lies instead of God's truth.

At that moment, I knew I had to at least try to make a better life for myself and my daughter. But then, other thoughts and emotions swirled viciously in my head like, "Well, maybe Jackson can change" and "There has to be a reason he acts this ways towards me isn't there...couldn't he get help and change?"

Yes, that was true but he had to change himself.

I had to get me and my baby into a safe place first, and, if Jackson wanted us back and wanted to restore his family, he would be the one that had to change himself – not dragging us along, destroying us both emotionally and physically.

All I knew at that moment was that I had to do my part and try. I couldn't fix Jackson anymore – I couldn't cover for him. This was no life.

A fresh determination directed my angry steps.

I had walked about a mile when the cop who was apparently helping Jackson change his tire spotted me and Samantha. I saw him get into his police truck and start driving towards us as we got to the beginning of the weigh station turn off.

When he got close, I recognized the policeman. In fact, Jackson and I had both gone to high school with him – Tony

Freeman was his name and he was a great guy.

He rolled down his window.

"It's way too cold for you and that baby to be out in the cold," he said at first.

"Yes, I very well know that," I snapped back, my teeth now chattering from the cold.

Then he recognized me.

"Rose, is that you? I thought Jackson was alone. I had no idea you and Samantha were with him."

I assured him he had the right person.

"Ya'll come get in here where it's nice and toasty," Tony instructed me and Samantha, helping us in his police truck and cranking up the heat.

We thankfully put our frozen hands up to his heat vents, thawing them out.

"Ok, Rose – what's the story here? Did you all have a fight or something? Tony asked friendly yet professionally. "I have to know what's going on."

I took a deep breath as I watched my husband changing his tire just a hundred yards before me. For a minute, Jackson stood up, pretending he was taking a break from the tire and glared at me right in my eyes. He knew he had broken even his own code and allowed his wife and daughter out of his sight, and now we were in the protected safety of a police truck.

He was losing power, and that angered him, so he tried to control me through manipulation.

For a moment after that incredibly glaring glance from my husband, my fresh determination was watered down. I almost just rattled off a half-hearted excuse to Tony to assure him that we were fine, go home and take the abuse one more night from Jackson and hope against hope that me and Samantha and my family were all alive the next day.

However, I felt a renewed strength well up in me. If for no one else but Samantha, I had to try.

"Tony, these are the hardest words I've ever had to say but I have to say them, do you understand?"

"Sure, Rose, go ahead."

"I know Jackson shows a good face in public, but he is an incredibly abusive husband and I am very afraid for my life and my family's life. This is the only chance I've had to get help and I'm asking for your help right now. Please believe me."

"Rose, I've known Jackson my whole life and I've never seen any indication that he could be abusive."

"Yes, I know Tony. That's how good he is at hiding it."

My determination grew stronger. This was my only chance and I needed proof.

I pulled my leggings just up enough to where Tony could see the bruise on my thigh.

"He did this just last night, and that's just the tip of the iceberg to what he has done," I told him. "Plus he left me and Samantha out here in 5 degree weather."

Seeing the proof, Tony's eyes turned very concerned, like maybe he believed me.

Tony told me he had just been through a special domestic violence workshop on the police force so it was fresh in his mind. "I can put him in jail him tonight for that bruise and for child endangerment, but I'm not sure how long they will keep him but I will try my very best for you and Samantha I promise you that – and there's somewhere I can take you and Samantha tonight where you will be warm and safe if you will go."

I debated back and forth for the next two minutes. I had heard that the day you try to leave your abusive spouse is the very most dangerous day. I shivered at the thought of what he might do when he got out of jail.

Still, I had to try, but I was terrified for my safety and for the safety of my family –

and now, for the safety of the cop, Tony Freeman.

"Tony!" I looked straight in his eyes. "If you confront Jackson right now, please be careful. He has a gun in his truck. I know you know what you are doing, but please be careful."

"I will Rose. I'm just doing my job tonight."

Tony got out of the truck casually and talked friendly to Jackson at first, I could tell from the truck cab as I watched the two finish up the tire as Jackson secured the last bolt with the lug wrench.

I rolled down my truck window an inch to hear their conversation.

Then, I heard it. Tony asked Jackson about my bruise and why he left us in the cold...wanted his side of the story.

Jackson's face became contorted with anger as quickly as he was confronted and didn't take time to answer Tony. Without giving Tony any reaction time at all, he swung the lug wrench with all his might at Tony's head, knocking him out cold on the pavement.

"Oh, dear God," I gasped, and rolled the window up in the police truck and locked the doors just in the nick of time before Jackson could jump in to grab me and little Samantha.

"What's Daddy doing?" she screamed and I held her tight to me and rested her head against my shoulder, trying to shield her from seeing the scene before her.

"It's gonna be ok, girl," I tried to reassure her, stroking her head with my right hand and kissing her head. "It's gonna be ok."

Jackson was raging at this point, screaming that he was going to break the window.

When he threw the lug wrench against the passenger side window, it felt like a thousand shards of glass hit both of us. I closed my eyes and continued to hold Samantha's head against my shoulder to protect us from the glass getting in our eyes.

Still, the glass was all over us and all over the cab of the truck.

Jackson jerked me out of the truck and the pieces of glass pierced my legs from the seat.

"God, please help us," I prayed in a scream.

That's when I heard it.

A gunshot rang through the cold night. Tony had come back to enough to grab his gun from where he lay on the pavement and shoot Jackson in the foot.

Jackson let go of me and shrieked in pain from the gunshot, falling on the pavement and grabbing his wound. "Tony, why in the world did you do that? You know I didn't do anything to the woman! She's a liar!"

"You stay right there on the ground!" Tony commanded. Now, he was back up on his feet standing over Jackson. "You won't be bothering anybody for a very long time, I guarantee you that."

Tony called for backup from another cop, asking him to call an ambulance for Jackson.

When the second cop car arrived, Tony escorted me and Samantha to the back of the cop car to keep us warm.

As I sat there holding my baby girl in the back of the cop car with pieces of glass still covering us watching Jackson being loaded onto the stretcher onto the ambulance, I knew one thing for sure – after this night, I would start a brand new chapter in my life, one that was violence-free.

I needed a miracle that night, and God had breathed confidence in me to be that miracle in my own life – along with the very special help of my old buddy, a cop named Tony Freeman, who I now considered an angel.

"Chloe's Worst – and Best – Valentine's Day"

Chloe felt like she was floating on air walking into Pisgah High School the morning of Valentine's Day. This was the first year she had a boyfriend to celebrate with and she had toyed in her mind for a week about what to give her new boyfriend, Landon.

Finally, she had come up with what she was pretty sure was the perfect Valentine's Day gift for a guy.

She worked three hours the night before on perfecting a dozen chocolate covered strawberries, homemaking the chocolate herself on the stovetop. "How could you go wrong with food for a guy?" she had commented to her mom the night before while meticulously dipping the strawberries in dark and white chocolate just right.

Her mother, Sandra, hadn't been quite as excited as she was the night before, sitting at the kitchen bar stool, watching her daughter work. "Have you prayed about this guy, honey? He's the first guy you've dated and you haven't known him very long and..."

"What are you talking about?" Chloe interrupted her mother, looking up from the strawberries surprised. "Landon is perfect."

"I just think you need to look around a little more, honey. He's not the only fish in the sea, that's all I'm saying."

"You're really busting my bubble here, Mama."

Her mom raised her hands in surrender. "It was bad timing, sweetie. I'm sorry. I just don't want to see you get hurt."

With that stood up, her mom stood up and kissed her daughter on the forehead. "Enjoy your Valentine's Day, sweetie, really...I love you. I'm off to bed."

Chloe dipped the last strawberry in chocolate at 11 p.m. and placed Landon's gift in the refrigerator before going off to sleep herself for a few hours before her cell phone woke her up at 5:15 a.m.

There was a lot to do that morning before school.

Chloe showered and dressed in a pretty red sweater, her new American Eagle skinny jeans and boots and took extra care in applying her makeup and curling her hair.

She paired the strawberries with a dozen red, heart-shaped helium balloons she bought that morning when she rushed into the local grocery store floral section.

You're gonna feel like the most special guy at school, Chloe texted Landon early that morning at 6:15 a.m. He had read the text at 7:14 a.m., but, so far hadn't texted back and it was 7:45 a.m., exactly when they had agreed to meet at the front of the school to exchange gifts.

He had been acting kind of cold towards her the past week, but she was determined to pull him back in to being the incredibly sweet guy he had been in early January when he first asked her out one day totally randomly in their second block English class.

Valentine's Day was just the day to get back on track romantically.

She couldn't believe he had ever even noticed her. Landon was one of the most popular football players in their high school junior class and she was the editor of the school newspaper and on the quieter side – pretty much on different sides of the tracks in the high school social life.

He had shocked her, really.

"Hey pretty girl, what you working on?" Landon sat down out of the blue in the empty desk in front of her at the end of class one day when the students were supposed to be working on the outline for their junior English research paper due in March.

He wore a white t-shirt, jeans, hiking boots and a camouflaged ball cap. He was tanned even in January and his rugged good looks and piercing green eyes totally caught her off guard.

She was speechless.

"So you're just gonna ignore a guy?" Landon was teasing now, grinning at her flirty.

"Umm...I was thinking about what to write my research paper on."

She was well aware that her cheeks were probably fire engine red.

"Well, what you come up with?" Landon was the poster boy for confidence and charm.

"I'm thinking about researching how people in the mountains survived the Great Depression. How they were self-sufficient...stuff like that."

"That sounds good." Now Landon was turned all the way around in the desk, his tanned, muscled arms on the back of the desk with his chin propped up on his arms.

Chloe noticed how his soft brown hair curled adorably around his ears.

"How'd you get that idea?"

Chloe's voice was shaking. "Just thought it would be interesting to research that part of history and I know a few people I could get some first-hand quotes from so...anyways, I just think it would be interesting."

Interesting...yeah, she had said that twice. *Oh, I'm mumbling now...get it together Chloe,* she thought to herself. *You're the one he's not going to find interesting if you don't quit rambling.*

"Well, how about we go out for a steak tonight and you can tell me more about it?"

What? A steak? Out to eat?

"Are you...uhh...are you asking me out?" Chloe clicked her pen nervously and finally stammered the question.

"If you will go, sweet girl." He grinned, flawlessly. "I've been noticing you here lately. You're one of the sweet ones."

Chloe couldn't believe what she had just heard. She had never even been on a date with any guy, and Landon had just asked her out?

"Sure, I guess so." It wasn't the classiest answer, but it was the best she could come up with under the circumstances.

Two very popular girls to Chloe's left, Sarah and Sadie, heard the whole conversation from the next row of desks and looked at each other in total shock. Sadie already pulled her iPhone out on her lap out of sight from their teacher to text the latest gossip.

"Sounds like a date. I'll pick you up at six?" Landon was on his feet.

"Okay." When Chloe heard the shrill bell ring signaling the end of class, she felt like she was waking up from a dream, but it was real and she couldn't believe her good fortune.

The two spent that night going out to eat at Canton's Sagebrush restaurant and were almost inseparable during the month of January, taking walks together around the Canton walking trail when the weather allowed and studying at the Waffle House together over hash browns and coffee on cold nights.

"Can I kiss you goodnight, girl?" he had asked Chloe, one cold January night on her front porch when he dropped her off after a late study date, tugging a strand of dark brown hair around her ear.

It was her first kiss, a little clumsy at first on her part, but Landon made it wonderful all at the same time.

After that kiss, Chloe ended up letting Landon have her idea of the Great Depression research paper and even helped him interview his grandparents for first-hand quotes and write the rough draft of his paper.

After all, he's been an angel to me...it was the least I could do to help him out, she had reasoned.

Chloe's phone finally dinged loudly at 7:57 a.m., interrupting her thoughts of the dreamy last six weeks with Landon.

It was Landon texting. *Hey, I'm running late this morning. Can I just see you in class?*

Chloe's high spirits of the morning deflated as much as if she had popped one of the dozen balloons she held outside of the school, now looking pretty stupid with no one to give them to. *Gee, thanks Landon. No "Happy Valentine's Day" or anything?* Chloe thought to herself.

Something was off. Landon just wasn't acting like himself.

Chloe hoped for the best. That's the way she was – always looking for the best in people.

Maybe he is just running really late and wants to surprise me in class?

Chloe decided that must be it and walked up two levels of stairs and down the hallway to her first block Algebra class, all the way carrying her homemade chocolate covered strawberries and balloons.

Katy, sitting in the back row of Algebra class, giggled when she walked in, pointing at the latest buzz on social media on her iPhone and showing it to her friend Elizabeth.

Both girls busted out laughing at whatever was on their phones.

"Oh my gosh, she's being a little extra with all the balloons, don't you think?" Katy had lowered her voice and turned towards Elizabeth with her hand over her cheek, but was still loud enough for Chloe to hear every word.

Clearly, the girls were making fun of her.

Then, after a minute, Elizabeth went quiet. "Should we tell her? I mean, I kinda feel bad for her, you know?" she asked Katy. "Like, if it was me, I would want to know."

"You're too nice Elizabeth!"

Then, Katy had another idea.

"Ok, let's tell her real quick before the bell. Then I can totally film it when she confronts Landon. It'll make a great story for Snapchat."

Elizabeth and Katy quickly got up and sat down in the desks next to Chloe.

Katy went first. "Hey I really liked your story in the newspaper about making the cafeteria food better...that food is really nasty."

"Thanks...I guess." Chloe wasn't too impressed with Katy's fake small talk.

Then, Elizabeth took over the conversation. "Look, Chloe. We just wanted to show you something we saw on Facebook this morning."

"Do you have Facebook?" Elizabeth asked.

"No I don't. Too much drama for me and I have too much to do with the newspaper. Why?"

Elizabeth looked around for their teacher. They only had five minutes before the bell rang. "Well, I really am sorry to be the one to show you this, but if it was me, I would want to know."

With that, Elizabeth handed Chloe her iPhone, open to Landon Tyson's Facebook timeline where he was tagged at 7:30 a.m. by Sadie Jones.

Chloe stared dumbfounded at the screen in front of her. Sadie had kept her post brief but it spoke loud and clear: *Absolute sweetest promposal EVER!!! #isaidyes #howcouldinot? #prom2019.*

The sole picture was of Sadie and Landon standing outside of his black Ford pickup with Sadie holding a box of donuts and a white poster with colorful letters between them that read: *"I DONUT know I could be any happier than if you would go to Prom with me?"*

Landon had asked Sadie to Prom? How in the world did he have the nerve to do this to her on Valentine's Day? Chloe's mind swirled as reality sank in.

Her heart sank to the floor and her face went pale as a ghost.

"Awww, I really am so sorry." Elizabeth tried to be nice, putting a hand on Chloe's right knee. Even Katy felt a little bad for Chloe.

Then Chloe glanced the post's comments.

Sadie's mom had commented first: *Oh my stars how precious...we must go dress shopping!*

How SWEET is that?!?!, Let's double date Sadie!! and *Forget the prom...I just want those donuts!* were among the other 32 comments.

Then Chloe saw the comment stopped her cold: *Wasn't he dating that Chloe girl like last week? The newspaper chic?*

If that comment was cold, the replies to that comment felt sub-zero to Chloe's heart.

Sadie had been the first to reply. *You mean the newspaper nerd? Landon was only hanging out with her so she could help him with his research paper!*

A friend commented: *Sadie that's so mean!*

Oh, well, I'm just keeping it real. He just had to ace English to play football next year so whatever...

Chloe had seen enough when the bell rang to begin Algebra.

"Okay girls, cell phones up for the rest of class and do not have them out again or I will take them for the rest of the day." Mrs. Jenkins meant what she said and Katy and Elizabeth immediately walked back to their desks and put both their phones in their backpacks and class began.

As Mrs. Jenkins asked for homework to be turned in from the night before, Chloe wanted the floor to swallow her up. A mixture of total embarrassment and total fury flooded her mind and she felt like she might throw up during the entire class.

God, please help me somehow...I can't get through this without you today, she prayed, fighting full-blown tears. She wanted to cry, but she was too mad to cry right now.

Immediately, a verse came to mind that she had memorized in church as a child: *"Trust in the Lord with all your heart and lean not on your own understanding. In all your ways acknowledge him and he will direct your paths."*

I'm trying to, but this is just really hard, Chloe thought. *I don't know how I'm going to make it through this day without dying of embarrassment.*

As soon as Algebra was over, Chloe collected her strawberries and balloons and withstood a multitude of snickers and funny looks as she made her way over to the next building for English class – the class where she was forced to see Landon.

Landon was the last person she wanted to see right now, especially with Katy and Elizabeth almost at her heels. If they wanted a show for their social media post, she wasn't going to give them one...not right now anyway.

As soon as she rounded the corner towards her class, she noticed a mass of long blonde hair and saw Sadie standing outside the door, still gloating over her poster and showing it to several girls.

"Hey Chloe...who are all those balloons for?" Sadie asked her sarcastically as she walked in the door.

Chloe walked right by without saying a word and sat in her normal seat.

Landon walked in thirty seconds late and glanced at Chloe without even getting a reaction in return.

At the end of class, Landon caught Chloe in the hall.

"So is it true, Landon? Were you just with me for the research paper? Was this just all about football?"

"I guess...but I really didn't mean to hurt you..."

"Well you have." This time, Chloe couldn't hold back the tears, standing right in front of him with what was supposed to be his gift.

"Listen Chloe, I didn't mean for you to find out like this today with Facebook and all...I really didn't."

"So you didn't want to tell me now...you just wanted to string me along for another month till the final paper was turned in is that it?"

Landon couldn't even look at her in the eyes. He knew he was busted.

"You know, if you just needed help on an English paper, there are tutors you know. You didn't have to do this to me."

It was a long shot, but charming Landon had an idea. "So does that mean we can still hang out and study, if I pay you for being my tutor?"

"No Landon, that's ok...finish your paper yourself."

With that, Chloe marched off to her car during her lunch break, tossing Landon's gift and all the balloons in the back seat of her Ford Taurus in the student parking lot before she sat down in the driver's seat to call her mom to tell her what happened.

"Oh sweetie, that's terrible. I'm so very sorry."

After school, she slouched on the couch in her living room, staring at a dozen balloons and stuffing herself with chocolate covered strawberries.

"Want a strawberry?" Chloe asked her mom after about 15 minutes of sitting on the couch and crying on her mom's shoulder. "If you don't eat some, I'll sit here and eat all of them myself."

"Sure thing...they do look delicious." Her mom ate the chocolate end of one strawberry. "Wow these are fantastic!"

"Landon sure missed out today...on a great gift...and a great girl and don't you forget that!"

"Everybody was laughing at me today, Mama. I made a total idiot of myself! I should have known Landon wasn't interested in a girl like me."

"Landon didn't deserve a girl like you if you ask me!" Her mom put her hands over Chloe's hands.

"Chloe, listen to me. You are beautiful and smart and interesting and you've got to hold your head up more and believe in yourself. God made you unique and special and God has somebody special out there for you. It obviously wasn't Landon because he didn't see you for who you are, but there's somebody out there."

Chloe appreciated her mom trying to cheer her up, but she just wasn't feeling it yet.

"Thanks Mama." Chloe tried to sound appreciative even though she couldn't even attempt to sound upbeat as her mom started preparing two roast beef sandwiches and chips and dip for both of them.

Then Chloe thought of the verse again. "You know what verse came to mind today after I found out all that about Landon?"

"I don't know, which one?" Her mom topped the roast beef with provolone cheese as she talked.

"The one I learned in Sunday School when I was a kid, the one from Proverbs that says '*Trust in the Lord with all your heart and lean not on your own understanding. In all your ways acknowledge him and he will direct your paths.*'"

"Those are very wise words, Chloe. I'm so glad God brought them back to your mind on a day like today."

"Yes, I sure needed something today with the day I had." Chloe didn't realize how hungry she was and quickly devoured the roast beef sandwich, sitting at the kitchen bar with her mom.

Then Chloe looked around the adjoining living room. "What are we going to do with all these balloons?" Chloe questioned her mom. "Like I seriously need to get these out of our living room so I won't think about this really crazy day."

"Okay I have a great idea, Chloe!" Her mom stood with purpose, looking at all the balloons. "Let's do what that Bible verse says."

Chloe wrinkled her nose in confusion. "I'm not following?"

"The verse says to acknowledge God and he will direct your paths, right?"

Chloe nodded. "Right."

"Well, we have all these balloons and the Bible already tells us to look after the sick so I say let's go give the balloons to the sick in the hospital. It'll be a win-win. The hospital patients will surely love the surprise gifts and it will get you out of the house – it's perfect."

Her daughter wasn't convinced. "I don't know...I'm really not in the mood to go visiting anybody right now. I've been crying all day."

"Would you rather sit here feeling sorry for yourself or would you like to do something about this and make someone's day out there?"

Chloe had to admit her mom had a good point, and she sure didn't have any other plans for the Valentine's evening.

"Okay, you got me. I'll go."

With that, Chloe washed her face and applied new makeup and piled into her mom's SUV with the balloons and were soon on their way to the county hospital, Haywood Regional Medical Center.

Once they walked through the circular hospital doors, her mom asked the volunteers if there were any patients who might need an extra lift – maybe someone who hadn't received any visitors?

The volunteers informed her mom that they couldn't give out that information due to confidentiality issues but they were welcome to visit whomever they would like.

On the elevator, her mom suggested they visit the cardiac wing. "Heart balloons for heart patients on Valentine's Day – that sounds fitting, don't you think?"

"Sounds good to me."

So the plan was set.

"These people are gonna think we are a little weird, Mama. Do you think this is a good idea?" Chloe was beginning to lose her confidence as they walked down the hospital hallway.

"Trust me, they will love it." Her mom knocked on the first door and a frayed looking 30-something mother opened the door. Her daughter, 5-year-old Jessica, was hospitalized after a setback with a heart defect she was born with, they quickly learned.

"Happy Valentine's Day, Jessica," Chloe commented to the young girl as she handed her the first red heart-shaped balloon.

The little girl grinned from ear to ear and held on tight to the string, tapping the balloon back and forth. "Look mommy!"

At that sight, Chloe smiled genuinely like she hadn't smiled all day.

"Wow, Jessica had just been talking about she had missed handing out Valentine's cards to her classmates in kindergarten and she was so upset to miss Valentine's Day and now she got to have Valentine's Day right here in the hospital – thank you both so much!" Jessica's mother was almost in tears as she hugged Chloe and Sandra.

"You're welcome," Chloe and her mother chimed.

In the middle of handing out the next ten balloons as they walked down the hallway to various very appreciative heart patients, young and old, Chloe stole a look at her mom. "Okay. I have to admit you were exactly right. I'm already feeling better."

"That a girl – I just had a feeling about this."

Finally, with just one balloon left, Chloe knocked on the door this time. With no answer, she almost decided to move on to the next room when she heard a man call from the hospital bed, "Is that you Lane?"

"No sir, it's not Lane." Chloe wasn't sure what to say next. "We're just passing out some Valentine's gifts. Can we come in?"

"Come on in," the man said.

As soon as he saw the balloon, the man brightened noticeably. "Well, hello there young ladies. Come on in."

Chloe went about introducing herself and her mom and tied the balloon on the end of the man's hospital bed. In five minutes, they learned the brief life history of the man. He had been a pastor in Waynesville for 40 years and was recovering from a serious heart attack he had suffered a week ago.

"I'm so used to doing the visiting as a preacher so I'm not used to being on the other side of the fence so this is a real treat."

The man looked weak but his eyes shone bright. "That was mighty kind of you both."

Chloe could tell he was genuinely touched as she tried to say goodbye.

"You don't have to leave so quickly. Please sit down and talk for a bit." So, Chloe and her mom sat in uncomfortable hospital chairs and chatted with their new friend with the name of Charlie, they learned.

"Tell me about yourself," Charlie asked and Chloe began to tell him how she had just turned 17 and a junior at Pisgah High School and how she was the editor of the school paper.

"You seem to be a mighty sweet little girl, Chloe. I was just telling my grandson Lane yesterday how he needed to find a sweet girl."

"Well, that's pretty neat." Chloe glanced at her mom and her mom couldn't help but grin in a motherly "Didn't I tell you so?" way.

Charlie proceeded to tell Chloe and Sandra how his 19-year-old grandson was attending Fruitland Baptist Bible College and was in his first year, studying to be a pastor.

"Lane is supposed to be here shortly to stay with me for the evening. In fact, I thought that was Lane knocking when you all came to the door."

About that time, a very handsome, tall young man knocked quickly on the door then walked on in, still carrying his school books with his Bible right on top. Chloe guessed he planned to sneak in some studying while camping out at the hospital for the evening. He had the bluest eyes Chloe had ever seen, she couldn't help but notice.

"Hey Grandpa, how are...." Lane stopped himself.

"Oh, I didn't know you had company Grandpa."

Charlie took the lead.

"Lane, this is Sandra and her daughter, Chloe." Lane cordially and genuinely shook both women's hands. "Very nice to meet you both."

"They are out cheering us sick folks up with some Valentine's balloons – wasn't that mighty kind of them?"

"It sure was," Lane answered his grandfather, sitting his books and Bible down on the window shelf and making himself comfortable in the recliner beside his grandfather. "Very kind for sure."

Then, Chloe noticed something she never expected. On the very top of Lane's brown study Bible was a square sticker with the scripture verse that read: *Trust in the Lord with all your heart and lean not on your own understanding. In all your ways acknowledge him and he will direct your paths. Proverbs 3:5-6*

Chloe smiled big at Lane. Whether it might be a new friendship or something more with Lane, she was convinced that God had indeed directed both of their paths – causing their paths to cross this chilly Valentine's evening in an unlikely hospital room.

Suddenly, she had a feeling that when she looked back on the Valentine's Day of 2019, it wouldn't be such a bad day after all.

"The Blizzard of 1993 Kiss"

Friday, March 12, 1993

Heavy snow was in the forecast for all of Western North Carolina and beyond that Friday, March 12, 1993 when 30-year-old Andy Wilkes woke up to his blaring alarm clock at 6:45 a.m., already anxious to go through with his plan for that day – and that night.

He was going to give in.

He was finally going to sleep with the pretty blonde bank teller who he had been flirting with for over a year during his increasingly regular stops at the bank.

Leah was her name and she was a stunning 25-year-old – blonde hair, blue eyes as deep as the ocean, an incredible dancer's body and a sweet smile.

The two had quickly worked out a plan for a romantic weekend quietly and discreetly during what appeared to be a normal banking transaction when she slipped him this note on scratch paper: "Don't you need some cash for a snowy weekend with me?"

Then, below those words, she had written her Asheville address, short directions and phone number.

The idea had been Leah's – but Andy didn't try to stop her.

Andy would find some errand he had to quickly run in Asheville – some excuse he could tell his wife, Cassie – and then he could just happen to get snowed in "accidently." He would pick Leah up at her house in Asheville in his four-wheel drive truck, and then the two of them would take off to the hotel.

Maybe it would be just for the night – maybe, if he was lucky, he could string this out for the whole weekend.

Cassie wouldn't like it when he called from the hotel in Asheville, but what could she really say if he was snowed in? Cassie had always hated driving in the snow so there was no way she would try to drive out to Asheville. He would pacify Cassie, tell her a few words she wanted to hear, and assure her he would be home as soon as he could get there.

Cassie would tough it out in the snow at home or maybe spend the night with her mother next door, and he...well, he would find a night of comfort with Leah – and

Cassie would never, ever know anything ever happened.

Leah had promised her secrecy. It was a solid plan and he had left no stone unturned.

Now, he just had to come up with an excuse – and go through with it.

Cassie had already left that morning for early morning duty at the elementary school in Bethel where she worked as a teacher's assistant, so he showered a bit longer than usual, lathering body wash on himself, then toweled off.

Looking in the mirror, he liked to think he had kept up his football body.

He dressed in dark blue jeans, a checked long sleeve dress shirt, a winter vest and leather dress shoes for his "Casual

Friday" workday at Johnston High School in Canton where he was a World History teacher.

He sprayed body spray on generously. *Leah likes this body spray...she had commented on how good it smelled last week at the bank*, he remembered.

Since he couldn't actually pack a bag so Cassie wouldn't suspect anything, he would grab more body spray and a few other things before he checked into the hotel, he decided, checking his wallet to make sure he still had the cash he had stashed away for the weekend.

The three $100 bills were safely tucked in a side pocket of his wallet, along with Leah's address and phone number.

As he started to bound out the door, he glanced at the red blinking light with a "1" on the answering machine, signaling there was one message neither he nor Cassie had listened to yet.

Who would call this early in the morning? Andy couldn't imagine who would have called, but figured they had called while he was in the long shower.

He pushed the "Play" button.

His mother's concerned, muffled voice came over the machine. "Andy, this is your mother. Andy...your Grandma has pneumonia so they are going to watch her for a few days. She should be okay but, if you can, do you mind going by before this snow comes in? She's at Asheville Regional

Hospital in 305. She would love to see you if you can. Love you. Be careful out there."

Click.

Andy hated himself for almost grinning at the grim news about his Grandma, but the timing couldn't have been better if he had written a script himself.

It was the perfect excuse.

Andy saved the message on the answering machine so that Cassie could hear it when she got home from work so she wouldn't have any reason to doubt his excuse.

"Bingo," Andy said, throwing a coat on to walk out to his truck.

He felt a twinge of guilt echo through his heart when he passed he and Cassie's wedding picture by the front door. Cassie, with her flowing brown hair around her and her green eyes sparkling, wearing her white wedding dress.

"I tried it your way God and it's not working," Andy said out loud, looking at the picture of the two of them smiling wide. "Cassie doesn't love me anymore...I think it's about time I tried it my way."

With that, he slammed the front door and cranked up his blue 1989 Chevy truck.

He turned the radio up. Garth Brooks was jamming. "*'Cause I've got friends in low places where the whiskey drowns and the beer chases my blues away and I'll be okay. I'm not big on social graces, think I'll slip on down to the oasis. Oh, I've got friends in low places.*"

That was more Andy's frame of mind that morning instead of thinking about the wedding picture.

He cranked up the music a little louder to drown out his lingering hesitations.

"Well, I guess I was wrong. I just don't belong. But then, I've been there before. Everything's all right. I'll just say goodnight and I'll show myself to the door. Hey, I didn't mean to cause a big scene. Just give me an hour and then. Well, I'll be as high as that ivory tower that you're livin' in 'cause I've got friends in low places..."

Andy was singing loudly now, pounding his fist against the steering wheel as he drove.

Nothing like some good Garth Brooks to get stuff off my mind, he reasoned.

Walking into the high school, he tried to focus on his students, although his primary focus was on Leah.

"Mr. Wilkes, are we getting out of school early today?"

Three students had already asked him the question within the first five minutes of class.

"That's a possibility but I haven't heard anything yet," he told the students.

Get it together Wilkes, he thought to himself. *Just go into teacher mode.*

"Okay students, let's get our minds on history instead of the snow. There's learning going on today."

For the next three hours, Andy tried to focus with everything he had on his students, but even they could tell he wasn't quite present.

When the announcement was made at 11 a.m., he was relieved.

"Pardon the interruption, teachers, but I have an important announcement." Principal Hawkin's voice was loud and clear on the school intercom.

"With a foot or more of snow expected to fall tonight, we will be dismissing school immediately after lunch today. We will begin dismissing bus riders at 12:15. Everyone stay safe out there this weekend."

His student Chad stood up and threw his hands up in the air, "Sledding at my house tonight...who's coming??"

After a series of cheers from his students, Andy didn't see any need in going forward with the lesson. The student's minds were already on the early start to their weekend off – and his was too.

"Okay everyone, you can go ahead and pack up and get ready for lunch. Be sure to reach chapters 20 and 21 over this snow break and be prepared to discuss when you get back."

His class grumbled collectively.

Chad responded first. "Seriously Mr. Wilkes – reading over snow break?"

Andy put his hand on Chad's shoulder. "You'll be bored in no time and ready to get in some reading, Chad. It'll be good for you."

Chad rolled his eyes at the comment.

When his last two car-rider students were almost ready to be dismissed, he used

his classroom phone to make a call to
Cassie's school.

"Good morning, Riverdale Elementary
School," the receptionist answered.

"Hi this is Andy Wilkes. Could I speak
to my wife, Cassie please? She's an assistant
in first grade."

"Sure, Andy, how are you? Haven't
seen you at church lately."

Keep your nose in your own business,
Andy thought.

"I'm good, Sharon. Just been busy
lately. Can you send me to Cassie please?"

"Sure, I'll transfer you now."

"Thanks."

In about a minute, Cassie's voice came
over the line with about twenty excited first
graders talking loudly in the background.

"Mrs. Robert's room. This is Cassie."

"Hey it's me."

"Sorry I'm having trouble hearing...Zeke your bus is next. I will let you know, just wait right there...and button up your jacket it's very cold out there..."

Obviously, the kids were taking Cassie's attention, just like everything else in her life lately, Andy thought as he listened to the buzz at the elementary school.

Then, Cassie was back on the line.

"Sorry about that it's a little crazy around here with early dismissal. I'm sorry...who is this?"

Andy spoke up louder.

"It's Andy, you know, your husband."

Andy's voice was dripped with sarcasm.

"Oh, hey."

Cassie used to be happy to hear his voice. Now her voice seemed flat at best.

"Hey, Grandma's in the hospital with pneumonia. I'm gonna go see her real quick before I come home. Mom left a message this morning on the answering machine."

"Do you want me to ride out there with you?"

Andy hadn't thought about that question.

"No it's ok I'll just meet you at home."

Cassie pressed again.

"I'll be out of here probably in about an hour. I just have to wait with a few of the kids for their parents to get here and then I can go."

"Really, it's ok I'm not going to stay long." Andy was growing impatient with the questions.

"Ok, whatever."

Kids yelled in the background. "Mrs. Wilkes, Jason hit me again can you tell him to stop?"

"Listen, I've got to go. I'll see you at home."

The phone clicked before Andy could even respond, then his last two students were dismissed and, within five minutes, Andy was back in his Chevy truck on his way to Asheville Regional Hospital to make a very quick stop in room number 305.

"Phone call number one in the books, phone call number two at the hotel and I'll be scotch free," Andy expressed loudly to himself and turned up the radio again.

"Time to jam out a little."

The first snowflakes appeared about the time country group Alabama's newest song – a chilling ballad called "Once in a Lifetime" – rang melodically though his truck stereo speakers.

Andy wasn't paying much attention to the words at first, and then he heard the words: *"You hold the Queen of Hearts and if you gamble on a diamond win the dealin' starts. You stand to lose it all as the cards begin to fall and the lesson learned is hard. You're only dealt the Queen of Hearts once upon a lifetime."*

"Ok, this is definitely not the song I need to hear right now," Andy mused.

"So if you're taking chances, know the chance you take. A broken heart's a high price to pay. Foolish ways will make fools of the wise and the best things seldom come along twice. Once upon a lifetime. You know that you've been blessed when you hold your first born tenderly against your chest and through the innocence you see the value of a family. And you feel a special bond that only comes along once upon a lifetime. So if you're taking chances, know the chance you take. A broken heart's a high price to pay. Foolish ways will make fools of the wise and the best things seldom come along twice. And people only find love like yours and mine once upon..."

Andy had heard enough. "Enough of this," Andy shouted as he switched the radio channel to some 1980s hard rock.

Def Leppard's "Pour Some Sugar on Me" blared, but even Def Leppard couldn't drown out his wife's face now.

A vision of the first time he kissed Cassie flashed through his mind, completely involuntarily. They were seniors in high school and he was a football player and she a bubbly cheerleader. They were regional football champions that year and, after the big win, he leaned over to Cassie under the stadium.

"I think this calls for you to finally kiss me," Andy had said happily, kissing Cassie firmly on the lips and smiling big, still over the moon about the win.

Cassie beamed. "What should we call this kiss?"

"I don't know – do you have to name kisses?" Andy asked.

"Well, I do." Cassie was an unusual girl, so happy and full of life and energy.

"I think we should call that our 'Championship Kiss.'"

So, it was settled – an executive decision had been made. Their first kiss had been named the "Championship Kiss," and from then on out, Cassie had named many kisses.

Some were totally random, like a "Fence Kiss" when they were standing beside her fence at home watching her family's horses. Others were more formal, like their

"Engagement Kiss" and their "Wedding Day" kiss.

For all the kisses they shared, however, Andy couldn't remember one kiss that he had ever named.

Well, there hasn't been any kissing going on lately in my house, so just forget it, Andy thought.

These memories were grating at his nerves when he pulled up in the hospital parking lot, slammed his truck door, walked into the hospital, punched the number "3" button on the elevator and shortly found room 305.

"Hey Grandma," Andy greeted his grandmother as he walked in her hospital room.

She was sound asleep, but she stirred slightly at his words.

"Andy...so glad..." She could barely hold her head up. "Glad you....came." Then she tried to sit up in the bed to see her grandson.

"Grandma, don't worry about getting up, I just came by real quick to see you before the snow came."

"How much?" His grandmother's words were brief.

"Supposed to be a big one – kind of like the big ones you used to tell me about when you were young, Grandma."

"Be careful."

"I will, Grandma...you get some rest and I'll try to stop back by after this snow clears." Andy had his right hand on the door handle to leave.

Suddenly, his grandmother found sudden strength and her voice was clear. "Andy, how is Cassie?"

Why is every single thing reminding me of Cassie today? Andy was growing more and more irritated with the reminders.

"She's fine Grandma."

"I'm praying for you both today I wanted you to know that." His grandmother's weak voice from earlier couldn't have been stronger.

"Thank you Grandma, get some rest."

With that, Andy furiously stormed out of the hospital, ready to put anything to do with Cassie temporarily out of his mind.

It was 4:45 p.m. by then and snow was beginning to come harder when he made a pit stop at Wal-Mart to pick up a few things for the hotel. After picking out new body spray along with pajama pants, a travel toothbrush, toothpaste, deodorant, breath mints and mouthwash, he paid in cash, threw the receipt in the parking lot trash can, tossed the Wal-Mart bag in the floorboard of his truck, pulled out Leah's address and directions and started towards her place.

"Clear your mind, Wilkes – no one will ever know," Andy spoke out loud.

You will know.

It was like the Lord himself spoke those words in the cab of his truck, but Andy dismissed them.

"No one is going to change my mind now," Andy said as he turned on High Mountain Drive, Leah's road.

At least three inches of snow had fallen by then and the freezing temperatures were causing the roads to freeze already, much sooner than Andy expected.

He skimmed the directions. *Six miles on High Mountain Road. Big log house on the right,* Leah had rapidly scribbled on the white scratch paper.

Three miles up, Andy realized Leah had failed to tell him the road was straight up and so winding and out in the middle of nowhere it seemed. When hc reached the top of the hill, the road went straight down.

"Ok, she didn't tell me about this either," Andy huffed.

His plans weren't going quite as expected.

Even his four-wheel drive Chevy truck wasn't any match for the patch of ice he hit going down the mountain road, sending his Chevy truck sliding off the side of the mountain, slamming against a giant oak tree.

Even with Andy's seat belt on, the force knocked his head against the driver's window, knocking him out cold.

When he woke up, his watch told him it was 10:03 p.m.

"Where am I?" he asked, looking around his truck and holding his head. He had a monstrous headache that throbbed throughout his body.

Andy pushed the truck door with all his might but the door wouldn't open at the angle it had landed against the tree.

He pulled a flashlight out of his glove box, rolled down the manual driver's side window and shined the flashlight on the snow.

"My goodness!" He moved his flashlight around to get a scope of the scene. "Oh, wow."

At least a foot of snow had already blanketed the woods in front of him and he quickly realized there was no way of getting his truck out of that place that night.

"What in the world am I doing out here?" Andy's head was pounding.

Then he saw the Wal-Mart bag. *Leah,* he suddenly remembered.

When Cassie flashed in his mind, he knew he was in so much trouble.

"Cassie is going to kill me," he muttered as blizzard wind blew in his truck.

Andy knew it couldn't be over 20 degrees out there and he had to find somewhere to go as quickly as possible.

Leaving the window down, he threw on an extra coat he had stashed behind the seat of his truck, grabbed the Wal-Mart bag and climbed out the driver's side window of his truck.

He needed hiking boots to trudge through this snow, not the leather dress shoes he had picked out that morning.

The wind seemed to blow harder and the snow got deeper the more he walked. He didn't see any houses anywhere in sight at first, but then, he thought he saw a light in the snowy wind.

Yes, Andy was sure it was a sole porch light maybe a quarter mile away down the mountain.

"Looks good to me." Andy struggled to walk as the wind almost took his breath.

The light went out.

"Please come back on, please." Andy felt delirious, trudging through snow as his head pounded.

Five more minutes went by, and finally the light came back on. Off and on the light went, but it stayed on just long enough for him to know which direction to walk.

Finally, Andy walked to the front door of the modest, small, A-frame log home.

With frigid bare hands, he knocked five times.

I just hope I don't get shot, Andy thought.

"Who is it?" A tall elderly man called gruffly, peeping through the living room curtains.

"My name's Andy...wrecked my truck out here."

The tall man opened the door. Looking to be around 80 years old, he still a full head of gray hair and was dressed in white thermal underwear from head to toe.

"Wrecked, huh?" The man looked Andy over, first noticing his red hands and face and looking down to his dress shoes.

"Hit a patch of ice and it sent my truck clear off the mountainside. I guess I was out for awhile and just woke up a little bit ago and saw your porch light."

"Come on in, son, and get in here by the stove and get warm."

Andy kicked off as much snow as he could off his shoes on the man's welcome mat and stepped inside to the cozy small log home, thankful to put his freezing hands up to the man's real wood fireplace.

"You've got this place toasty for sure," Andy commented, thawing out by the fire, looking around the fireplace mantle to see a centerpiece picture of an elderly woman with gray hair and kind green eyes, surrounded by multiple pictures of what looked like many children and grandchildren.

"I try to keep it that way if I can." The man shook Andy's still frigid hand. "My name's Chuck. Chuck Henry."

"Andy Wilkes, sir." Andy returned the handshake heartily. "Very nice to meet you and thanks for letting me in like this. I hope I didn't startle you too much."

"It's okay, son, if you had startled me too much, I would have taken care of that real quick like," Chuck shot back, pointing to his rifle propped by the front door.

The two men chuckled.

"No, I'm fine. I've just been turning the lights off and on for a little bit seeing how deep the snow was getting before I went to bed."

Then, Andy understood the porch light that just stayed on long enough for him to see the house.

"Well, I was sure glad to see your light on walking in that blizzard, sir."

Chuck nodded. "Well I guess there's a reason for everything isn't there?"

"Yes, sir."

"I have some leftover meatloaf if you want some." Chuck rummaged through his refrigerator. "And how about some hot chocolate to warm you up?"

Both sounded heavenly to Chuck. "Sounds wonderful, thank you very much."

Soon, Chuck returned from his kitchen with a paper plate full of meatloaf, green beans and mashed potatoes and a steaming cup of hot chocolate and sat down in the living room on the couch by the fire.

Andy took off his coat finally, sat the Wal-Mart bag down in front of him and made himself comfortable in the oversized recliner, quickly devouring his food like he hadn't eaten in a week.

As he ate, Chuck peered over Andy, noticing his clothing and how ill-equipped he was dressed for the snow, and then observed the plastic Wal-Mart bag and some of the contents that had spilled out. Chuck's eyes looked quizzically at the new pajama pants with the tag still on them and the other hygiene items.

"Where you from, Andy?" Chuck questioned.

"I'm from over in the Bethel community in Haywood County."

"So, tell me – what are you doing all the way over here not dressed for the snow and with new pajamas and deodorant and mouthwash and such you just bought?"

"Well, my grandmother is in the hospital and I came over this way to visit her....and...well..." Andy trailed off, not sure how to continue.

"This meatloaf is really delicious," Andy interjected, trying his best to change the subject.

"Listen, I was born at night but I wasn't born last night and I'm a whole lot smarter than I look." Chuck was kind but assertive.

"A man doesn't buy all that stuff to go see his grandmother and anyways the hospital's not anywhere near here. What are you doing over here?"

Andy wasn't sure what to say, and said nothing.

Chuck leaned forward knowingly at Andy. "You're somewhere you're not supposed to be, aren't you son?"

Andy didn't say anything for a solid minute.

Then he just simply looked Chuck in the eye and said, "Yes sir, I guess I am."

Andy didn't usually express himself too well to people, but there was something about Chuck and his kindness and the meal and being in a cozy log home away from anybody who knew him that made him suddenly to vent to Chuck, his newfound friend.

"Chuck, I'm 30 years old. I married my high school girlfriend Cassie when I was 22 years old, right out of college. We've been married eight years and it's just not working anymore."

Chuck nodded. "Okay, go on."

"When I first met Cassie she was a happy go-lucky girl...a cheerleader. She was happy all the time and now, she just nags me all the time – she nags me about going to church with her. I mean, I'm a Christian and all but she wants to go to church on Sunday morning and then on Sunday night and Wednesday night and she wants to have these small group marriage or whatever meetings at our house and I just don't want all these people up in my business like that. I mean, my Dad went to church twice a year –

on Easter and for Christmas – and my mother never complained about it. Why does Cassie have to complain so much? I'm a God-fearing man, don't get me wrong, but what's wrong with going to church twice a year?"

Andy stopped just long enough to devour another bite of meatloaf.

"Then she nags and nags about me walking with her. I just don't like to walk you know? It's just not something I like to do. Then she nags about me getting the yard done and flowers planted and it's just not my thing."

Andy took a sip of his hot chocolate and took a deep breath.

"She's gained about 20 pounds and we've just lost our romance I guess. We haven't made love in about two months and I'm just about fed up with her nagging. I just want her to go back to the girl I married, you know? Is that too much to ask?"

After his venting monologue, Andy looked at Chuck, expecting him to console him and take his side.

"Are you finished?"

"I guess...that's about it I guess. I could go into more but that's pretty much the story."

Andy gulped down a spoonful of mashed potatoes.

"The woman I was going to see is always complimenting me and so full of life and I wish Cassie was more like her."

Chuck stood up to replenish his hot chocolate. When he sat back down, he looked straight in Andy's eyes.

"Well, I would say son, it sounds to me you're being mighty selfish to me."

Chuck didn't mince his words.

Andy was thrown back. "Selfish?"

"Yes, you heard me right."

"How can you say I'm selfish?"

Chuck's words were direct. "You're just thinking about what you can get out of marriage – not what you can put into it."

"With all due respect sir, I don't think you know me very well."

"I think you're wrong about that," Chuck said. "First of all, Cassie is right about the Lord, A good marriage takes three – you and Cassie and God."

"I guess you have a point there," Andy conceded, and then Chuck pressed further.

"So, let me get this right, you married a socially, bubbly girl and you're complaining that she's now a socially, bubbly woman who wants people at your house? You're complaining that she's gained weight but you refuse to walk with her?"

If Andy wasn't trapped in this man's house, he would have stormed out the door, but he was basically a captive audience of one.

"And the things she's asking you to do? Go to church, walk with her, get to know a few people, plant some flowers? That sounds like pretty easy, cheap things to do to me."

Andy was getting beyond frustrated.

"You don't really know her – she's very hard to live with."

"Well, son, Cassie's not perfect, nobody is. But she sounds like a good woman to me."

Andy rolled his eyes.

"And to be honest, you don't sound like you've been a barrel of fun for her to be around either, if you want the truth."

"What would you know about a bad marriage, Chuck?" Andy almost couldn't believe his own bravery in asking the question to the man who had invited him into his home.

"It looks like you had a perfect family here...a beautiful wife, children and grandchildren. I guess you just had the perfect life."

With those words, Chuck stood up to his full six foot height and pondered lovingly at the picture of the woman on the center of the fireplace mantle for a minute or more.

When he turned to face Andy, noticeable tears welled in his aged eyes.

"Andy, let me introduce you to my late wife, Clara. I lost her last year to breast cancer."

"I'm very sorry for your loss, sir."

"Well, thank you. She was the greatest woman I've ever known," Chuck expressed nostalgically.

Chuck was still staring at the picture when Andy spoke up, "Why arc you telling me this, Chuck?"

"Well, I don't usually tell people this but I think you need to hear this Andy." Chuck sat back down on the couch.

"I was about your age when Clara walked into this very house and caught me right in the act with my secretary." Chuck eyes faded with the spoken words giving life to the 50-year-old memory.

"I've never seen a soul look so injured in my whole life as Clara looked in that moment."

Andy was shocked. "I'm sorry, Chuck...I would have never thought that."

"It was the stupidest mistake I've ever made," Chuck continued. "She had a heart of pure gold and, it took her awhile, but she took me back and loved me and I never wanted to even look at another woman the rest of my life."

"So you all worked things out...things were okay after that?" Andy questioned.

"She took me back and it was tough, but honestly, I think it was tougher on me than it was her."

Chuck looked unbelievably sad.

"Do you know how hard it is to look at the woman you love with all your heart for the rest of your life and know you broke her heart to pieces?"

Andy's tears spilled at this point.

"It's no fun, I know that," Chuck stated pointedly. "Andy I had to live with that for fifty years. To be honest, it still bothers me."

Andy was genuinely touched. "Thank you for sharing that with me, Chuck. I really do appreciate it."

"The grass ain't always greener on the other side, is it?"

"No sir, I don't see any green grass over here tonight," Andy chuckled as he flicked snow still stuck to his jeans, making Chuck smile too.

"Andy, I think the Lord brought you over here tonight, I really do."

Through tears, Andy shook his head in agreement.

"I think so too, sir," Andy finally choked out.

"Do me a favor, will you Andy?"

"What favor is that?"

"Go home and be real good...as good as you can be to Cassie and I promise you that she'll be good to you."

"It's a deal, Chuck," Andy promised Chuck as the two men shook hands and shared a great big, long bear hug in the living room.

"Speaking of Cassie, I don't really want to face her right now, but I need to call because I know she's going to be worried. Can I borrow your phone please?"

Chuck grabbed his phone off the base. "Sure thing. My daughter just got me one of these fancy cordless phones," Chuck said with a laugh, handing him the white cordless phone.

It was pushing midnight when Andy punched in his familiar home number, and then waited nervously as the phone rang.

Cassie answered on the first ring. "Hello?"

"Cassie, it's me, Andy."

"Andy, I've been worried sick about you! I've called everybody in your family and I even called the cops! Where are you?"

Andy cried at the sound of his wife's voice.

"Cassie, I wrecked and I hit my head and was out for awhile but I'm okay now."

"Are you sure you're okay? You sound like you are crying. Andy, where in the world are you?"

"I wrecked off High Mountain Road in Asheville. I've got to get my truck out when this snow clears," Andy answered, waiting for the backlash.

"What are you doing on High Mountain Road?" Cassie had an accusatory tone in her voice.

Andy hung his head in his left hand, holding the phone with his right hand, trying to figure out what to say.

"Cassie, I promise you I almost screwed up real bad and I'll have to tell you all about it when I get home but nothing happened I promise. I just want to tell you that I love you with all my heart and you're my 'Queen of Hearts' and you always have been."

"Andy are you really okay? Did you hit your head harder than you think?" Cassie asked on the other end of the line.

He hadn't been this expressive to Cassie in several years and she didn't know quite what to think.

"I promise you I'm fine. Better than I have been in a long time. Cassie I love you, do you know that?"

This time, Cassie was crying. "I love you too, Andy."

Cassie didn't know exactly how all the puzzle pieces had fallen together to bring her sweet husband back to her like this, but she silently thanked God for answering her prayers.

"Can I ask a favor, Cassie?"

"What is it Andy?"

"When I come home, can I give you a long kiss and name it?"

Cassie couldn't have been more shocked than if she had been handed a million dollar gift.

"What would you name it Andy?"

Andy was silent for about ten seconds.

"Are you still there, Andy?"

"Yes," Andy finally managed to get out through tears. "I want to name this one the 'Blizzard of 1993 Kiss.'"

Made in the USA
Columbia, SC
25 February 2022